DOUBLE TROUBLE ON VACATION

by Michael J. Pellowski

illustrated by Estella Hickman

*To the youngsters of
St. Jude Children's Research Hospital*

Published by Willowisp Press, Inc.
401 E. Wilson Bridge Road, Worthington, Ohio 43085

Copyright © 1989 by Willowisp Press, Inc.

Printed in the United States of America
10 9 8 7 6 5 4 3 2 1

ISBN 0-87406-424-4

One

"WE love you Kickapoo, oh, yes we do," I sang. "Lake Kickapoo, we love you!"

"Lake Kickaphew, we lub you," my three-year-old brother, Teddy, repeated the song I had made up. "Kickaphew! Kickaphew! Kickaphew!" he continued as he bounced up and down in the backseat of our station wagon.

"Knock it off, Teddy!" Randi, my twin sister, ordered. She looked up from the fishing magazine she was reading and stared at our brother. Randi had really gotten into fishing in a big way lately. She was excited about being able to do a lot of fishing during our stay at Lake Kickapoo. "Sit still! I'm trying to read," Randi ordered. "Besides, the name of the lake we're going to is Kickapoo—not Kickaphew!"

Trouble stopped bouncing and made a face at Randi. Trouble is our pet name for Teddy. I guess Teddy got his nickname the old-fashioned way—he earned it! Randi and I both love our little brother. But whenever there's a spill, a mess, or a disaster around our house, Teddy is usually the one who caused it.

Of course, Mom and Dad don't usually see it that way. They always blame us, Randi and Sandi, their look-alike daughters. Can you believe it! They call *us* the Trouble Twins.

I turned toward Teddy and smiled. "Randi's right," I said. "No more bouncing. And the name of the lake is Kickapoo, Teddy. It's an old Indian name. Can you say Kickapoo?"

"Kickaphew!" Teddy shouted grinning from ear to ear. "Kickaphew! Phew! Phew! Phew!" he repeated.

"Now see what you started by singing that stupid song?" Randi said to me.

"Can I help it if I like to sing?" I replied.

I looked out at the tall trees we were passing. I got to thinking about how Randi and I are different in a lot of ways, even though we're identical twins. We like different things. Randi's a better athlete, but I'm a better singer. I love romance novels, but all Randi ever likes to read is the sports page of the newspaper—and that fishing magazine she's drooling all over. I sometimes wear glasses, but she doesn't.

We even like different colors. I love pink and purple. And Randi's totally into red.

And if that's not enough, I'm a member of the Great Lovers of Woodlands club for girls. It's called G.L.O.W. Girls for short. Randi couldn't care less about the G.L.O.W. Girls.

In fact, G.L.O.W. is the main reason I was so thrilled when Mom told us we were spending a month of summer vacation at a cabin at Lake Kickapoo.

Lake Kickapoo is the national camp headquarters of G.L.O.W. Ms. Morgan, a teacher at our school and my local G.L.O.W. leader, will be at the G.L.O.W. camp over the summer. I was going to give a special speech on wildlife at the camp during our stay at the lake. If the speech was good enough, I would win an important G.L.O.W. Girl merit badge. I was dying to get that badge.

After a while, I took out my G.L.O.W. handbook and opened it to the wildlife section.

"Oh, no," groaned Randi, watching me open my handbook. "Here we go with that G.L.O.W. stuff again. If I hear one more word about that wildlife merit badge, I'll get car sick!"

Usually, I don't get too riled up about things. Randi is the one who flies off the handle. I can stand a lot of teasing, but when Randi insulted G.L.O.W., that was definitely too much.

I slammed my handbook shut. "Randi Daniels, you've pushed me too far," I huffed. "You know how much that merit badge means to me. All you care about is your stupid, slimy,

gross, bug-eyed fish!"

"That's enough!" cried Dad without taking his eyes off the road. "Randi and Sandi, stop bickering! If this is how you're going to act at the cabin, I'm glad I'm only going to be there on weekends."

"I'm sorry, Dad," I said.

"I'm sorry too, Dad," Randi said.

"Sorry, Sandi," she added, looking at me. "I didn't really mean what I said about G.L.O.W. I guess I'm just cranky from this long drive."

"Now, that sounds more like the Daniels family on vacation," said Dad.

I smiled and nodded. "We'll miss you, Dad," I said. "It won't be much of a vacation only seeing you on weekends. It's too bad you have to work during the week."

"Yeah," Randi said. "I wish we could spend the whole vacation fishing together."

"Don't worry, Randi," he continued. "I'm sure you'll find a fishing buddy soon. Lake Kickapoo is famous for its great fishing."

Dad looked in the rearview mirror and winked at me. He knew Randi's fishing buddy sure wouldn't be me. I hated fishing! Sticking wiggly worms on hooks to catch slimy fish would make me gag in about two seconds!

"Well," said Dad, "I'm just glad we were lucky enough to get a cabin at Lake Kickapoo when the other family canceled their reservation at the last minute."

"That's right," said Mom. "Otherwise, you guys would have had to spend the summer at home."

"Being home wouldn't have been so bad," Randi said. "At least that creep Bobbi Joy Boikin went away for the summer."

"Randi, don't call Bobbi Joy a creep," Mom said.

Bobbi Joy Boikin was the neighborhood bully. She was the biggest girl in our class at school. She always tried to boss people around. Randi and I tried not to pay attention to her. I think that's why Bobbi Joy disliked us.

"Did Bobbi Joy go to summer camp this year?" Dad asked.

"Nobody knows," I answered. "She just disappeared the week after school ended," I explained. "No one knows where she went."

"Let's forget about Bobbi Joy and talk about our vacation," Mom suggested.

"I hope the cabin is nice," I said.

"So do I," Randi said. "I don't want to have to hike to the bathroom."

That was the wrong thing to say.

"Batroom!" yelled Teddy. "I gotta go the batroom." He started bouncing up and down again.

"Oh, dear," Mom said. "I wish you hadn't reminded Teddy. Is it much farther?"

"Don't worry," Dad said. "Lake Kickapoo is just down the road." Dad turned our car off the highway and onto an old dirt road.

"Batroom!" Teddy yelled again as the car's wheels churned up clouds of dust. "I gotta go the batroom!"

Two

WE all piled out of the car and stormed into the cabin as soon as Dad got the front door unlocked. Then the mad hunt for the bathroom began. Luckily, Randi opened the right door on the first try. It really was a close call for Teddy.

"It sure is beautiful here," I said t o my sister after we wandered outside.

"It's awesome!" Randi answered.

We just stood by the car and looked around at the mountains, woods, and lake. Cabins dotted the gentle slopes that rise up from the water's edge. Out on the blue lake, sailboats and canoes bobbed up and down.

On the far side of the lake, I could barely

make out the little town and the nearby G.L.O.W. Girl headquarters.

"Isn't this romantic?" I asked Randi. "It's a perfect place for a romance novel."

"Huh?" she grunted. "I'm just wondering how the fishing is. Do you think the big ones are biting?"

I looked at Randi and just shook my head. She was about as romantic as a rusty old can filled with squirming worms.

"Hey!" shouted Dad as he came down the path from the cabin. "Does anybody want to help me and Teddy catch a frog?"

"Yuck!" I answered.

"Teddy wants a pet frog, and I promised to help him find one," Dad explained.

"Super," I mumbled. "Worms, fish, and frogs. This is going to be a great vacation!"

"Don't forget about skunks, snakes, and spiders," Dad joked as he began to unpack the car. Randi laughed, but I didn't think it was all that funny.

"Why don't you girls take a walk down to the lake?" Dad suggested. "We'll call you when lunch is ready."

In a flash Randi and I were off down the winding dirt path that led from the cabin to the lake. "This is great," I said when we reached the shore of Lake Kickapoo.

"It sure is," Randi replied, picking up a large flat stone.

"Watch this," she said. "I can skip stones like a pro." Randi reached back and fired the rock toward the water. But instead of skipping, the stone just landed in some reeds with a big splash.

"HEY!" yelled a voice from behind the reeds. "Knock it off! You'll scare away all the fish!"

Randi looked at me with surprise. I looked back at her and shrugged my shoulders. "I don't see anyone," I said.

"Me neither," said Randi. Then she called out, "I'm sorry! I didn't see you. In fact, I still don't see you."

"Wait a second, and I'll come out," the voice replied.

We heard a sloshing sound and saw the lake water near the reeds ripple. Out of the tall reeds came a canoe paddled by a boy who was around our age. He was tall and thin, with bushy hair the color of straw. In the canoe was a fishing rod and reel.

"Hi," the boy called. "You're new around here, aren't you? Are you on vacation?"

"Yes," I answered as he paddled toward shore. "We're spending four weeks here. I'm Sandi Daniels, and this is my sister Randi." I pointed at Randi. "She threw the stone that almost conked you."

"Sorry again," Randi apologized as the front of the boy's canoe touched the beach.

The boy looked at me. Then he looked at Randi. Then he looked back and forth at us.

"Holy frying flounder!" he shouted. "I must have been out on the lake too long!"

Randi and I both burst out laughing.

"We're identical twins," Randi explained.

"I'm Sandi," I added. "Randi is the one in the red football jersey."

"So, you're Sandi," the boy said pointing at me. "And you're Randi? Or, is it the other way around?"

He shook his head and scratched his yellow hair. "You two sure could make a guy think he was seeing double," he said. He unbuckled his life jacket and climbed out of his canoe.

"You should see our cousin Mandy," I said. "She looks exactly like us too."

The boy blinked in disbelief.

"Well, who are you?" asked Randi.

"Me? Oh! I'm sorry!" the boy sputtered. "I was so amazed that I forgot to introduce myself. My name is Walter Warren Wormsley III," he said. "But everybody around here just calls me Wormy. My family lives at Lake Kickapoo all year around."

"Wormy," I said. "That's kind of...well...sort of...a funny nickname."

"I like it," Randi said.

"Everyone calls me Wormy because I love to fish," he said. "And being named Wormsley has something to do with it, too."

"Do you like to fish?" asked Randi. I could see an excited look in her eyes. "I love to fish myself. Are there a lot of fish in this lake?"

"It's loaded," Wormy told Randi. "And I know all the best spots. I'll show you all the good places to fish."

Then Wormy looked at me. "Do you fish, too, Sandi?" he asked.

"No," I said quickly. "I'm more interested in animals. I'm going to give a speech on wildlife at the G.L.O.W. camp."

"Did you guys know that the annual Lake Kickapoo fishing derby is coming up?" Wormy asked. "You and your sister should enter the Junior team competition."

"That's a great idea," Randi replied quickly.

"Not on your life," I muttered to myself. "Hey, Wormy," I began, changing the subject.

"Is it hard to keep your balance in a canoe?"

"Nah," he answered. "It's easy. Hop in. I'll show you."

"Okay, I will," I answered. I carefully climbed into the beached canoe and made my way to the opposite end. I sat down and peered into the murky lake water. It was so cloudy I couldn't see the bottom.

"Here we go!" said Wormy. He got in and pushed off. The canoe slowly slid away from the shore. It rocked a bit.

"Gee, this canoe is kind of tippy," I said nervously as the boat began to bob and shake.

"You have to sit still, Sandi," Wormy warned as he picked up his paddle.

"I don't like this," I groaned, trying to get to my feet. And do you know what? I forgot G.L.O.W. Girl water safety rule number one—never stand up in a boat.

"Sandi, sit down!" Wormy shouted. But it was too late. Splash!

Over the edge of the canoe I tumbled, right

into the lake. And I wasn't even wearing a life jacket! That was G.L.O.W. Girl water safety rule number two—always wear a life jacket when you're in a boat.

"Help! Help! Help me!" I screamed as I splashed and splashed.

"Stand up, Sandi!" Wormy hollered. "The water's shallow."

"Huh?" I sputtered. I stood up. The water was barely up to my waist. Was I ever embarrassed! I felt like a complete nerd. I looked at Wormy sitting in the canoe, which was floating toward me. He was too polite to laugh, but Randi wasn't too polite to laugh.

She was standing on the shore, doubled over, about to explode with laughter. She had her mouth covered by her hands.

"Go ahead and laugh," I groaned. "I know I made a goof out of myself."

They were laughing so hard that I couldn't help laughing myself. I'm sure I looked pretty dumb. I sloshed my way to shore.

"I guess I'd better go change," I said as I stood there dripping wet.

"You're a good sport, Sandi," Wormy said as he beached his canoe again and stepped out. "Having the Daniels twins this summer at Lake Kickapoo should be fun—make that double fun!"

I started to walk toward the cabin. My water-logged sneakers sloshed and squeaked with every step I took.

"Up here we call a wet foot like that a soaker," said Wormy.

"Sandi got a soaker all over," joked Randi.

Then she said to Wormy, "Do you want to come over for lunch? Then you can meet our mom and dad and Trouble."

"Lunch sounds great," said Wormy. "But who is Trouble?"

"You'll find out," I promised as I squished and sloshed my way up the path.

"Yeah," said Randi. "Right this way for Trouble!"

Three

"HI, Sandi," Dad said when he saw me coming. "I was just about to call you for lunch." Then Dad noticed my clothes. "What happened?" he asked.

"I got a soaker," I replied. "That's what they call falling in the lake up here."

Then Randi and Wormy came up the path. "Dad, this is Wormy," announced Randi. "He's going to show me all the best spots to fish."

"His real name is Walter Warren Wormsley III," I said. "But everyone calls him Wormy. It was his canoe I fell out of."

"Is it okay if Wormy stays for lunch, Dad?" asked Randi.

"Sure," Dad replied.

Just then the cabin door flew open, and out raced Teddy. He zoomed over to us and stopped in front of Wormy. "Who you?" Teddy asked, pointing at Wormy.

"I'm Wormy," he said as he bent over to shake hands with Teddy. "Who are you?"

"He's our little brother, Teddy," I explained.

"This is the trouble we were telling you about," Randi said to Wormy. "Trouble is Teddy's nickname."

"Wormy," Teddy said. "Dat a good name. Maybe I name my pet froggie Wormy."

"Do you have a frog, Teddy?" Wormy asked.

"Not yet," Dad answered. "Teddy and I are going frog hunting right after lunch."

"There's a stream just behind your cabin that has lots of frogs in it," Wormy said.

"Thanks for the tip," said Dad.

Just then Mom opened the door and called us for lunch. When she saw me, she asked, "Sandi, what happened?"

"She got a soaker," Dad kidded.

"I fell in the lake, Mom," I said.

"Well, it's lucky you weren't wearing your glasses," Mom replied. "I think you'd better change clothes before lunch, don't you?"

I nodded and sloshed off toward the cabin.

"Sanee got a soaker," Teddy sang out. "Sanee got a soaker!"

After I changed, we all sat down to lunch. At the table, Teddy quickly showed how he got his famous nickname. First he spilled his moze. Moze is Teddy's word for milk. Part of the milk splashed into the potato chip bowl and got the chips all soggy. Teddy picked up one of the soggy potato chips and stuck it on his forehead.

"Teddy," said Dad, "take that potato chip off your head. That's not where it belongs."

Next Teddy ruined his sandwich. When he picked it up to bite it, the baloney slid out and landed on the floor with a loud splat! Lunch was one disaster after another thanks to Trouble. Poor Mom spent most of the time cleaning up after Teddy.

"Thank you for the lunch, Mrs. Daniels," said Wormy when we'd finished. "It was great."

Dad cleared the table, and then he and Teddy headed down to the stream. "Bye, everybody," Teddy called as they were leaving. "Now I gonna catch me some froggies."

"I'll help with the dishes," I said to Randi. "You can walk Wormy back to his canoe."

She winked at me and said, "Thanks, Sandi. I'll pay you back."

"Wormy seems like a nice boy," Mom said after Wormy and Randi had left. She washed, and I dried.

I nodded. "I think Randi kind of likes him," I replied. "He's cute, but he's not my type."

Mom laughed. "Any boy who likes to fish wouldn't exactly be your type."

I smiled and shook my head.

"Besides," Mom continued, "when was the last time you and Randi liked the same boy?"

I had to think way back to answer Mom's

question. The last time Randi and I liked the same boy was when Randi, our cousin Mandy, and I all had secret crushes on a boy named Christopher Miles. Wow! That caused a lot of problems.

"Hey," Mom said. "If you don't stop daydreaming, we'll never finish these dishes." I snapped out of my trance and went back to work. Before long the dishes were done.

"I'm going outside, Mom," I called as I headed for the door. I stepped out onto the front porch of the cabin. Dad and Teddy were nowhere in sight. And Randi hadn't returned from walking Wormy to his canoe.

I went to the car to get my G.L.O.W. handbook. I also took out a pencil and a small note pad. Just as I slammed the car door, Randi came up the path from the lake.

"Thanks for helping Mom," Randi said. "I'll take your turn with the dinner dishes."

"Wormy's pretty nice," I replied.

"He's cool," Randi answered. "I like him. He

sure knows a lot about fishing. He's taking me fishing tomorrow."

"I'm going to take a walk in the woods to make some notes for my wildlife speech," I explained. "Do you want to come?"

"Sure," answered Randi. "I'll tell Mom."

"Okay," I called as Randi raced off toward the cabin.

Minutes later, Randi was back. "Mom says not to get lost and to be careful," Randi instructed. "And she said to watch out for wild animals."

"We won't get lost," I told Randi as we started toward a path that led through some tall pine trees. "And we don't have to worry about wild animals, either. My handbook says there are no dangerous animals around here."

As we strolled through the forest, I made notes in my note pad about animal tracks and forest creatures we saw. We surprised a few squirrels, scared a chattering chipmunk, and even caught a glimpse of a fawn with its mother having lunch.

We were having such a good time that we didn't notice that we were getting pretty far away from the cabin. Deeper and deeper into the dark woods we went. We began to hear strange noises in the bushes and treetops.

"Are you sure there are no bears, wolves, or mountain lions around here?" Randi asked as she stopped and glanced around.

I gulped and shook my head. "The guidebook says we're perfectly safe," I whispered.

Suddenly, we heard a terrifying howl that chilled us right to the bone. The bushes near us began to rustle. Something growled! We were petrified with fear!

"W-wh-What's that?" sputtered Randi nervously.

"I-I-I don't know," I babbled as I cowered in my soggy sneakers. We began to tremble and shake. Something was in the bushes behind us. And we didn't know what it was!

"AARRGGHHH!"

Out of the bushes jumped a girl with frizzy red hair.

"Bobbi Joy Boikin!" I yelled.

"What are you doing here?" demanded Randi

"Boy! I sure scared you two turkeys," Bobbi Joy said laughing. Out of the bushes behind her came a boy we didn't know.

"That was a dirty rotten trick," Randi said.

"Ha-ha," laughed Bobbi Joy. "If you two weren't so stupid, you would have never fallen for it. Everyone knows there are no animals to be afraid of around here."

"What are you doing here, Bobbi Joy?" I asked, stepping between her and Randi. "We're here on vacation."

For a second Bobbi Joy didn't answer. Then she pointed at the boy behind her. "I'm visiting my cousin Jay-Jay Smith," she said.

Jay-Jay smiled. He was about our age and had reddish brown hair and blue eyes.

"I visit Jay-Jay every summer," Bobbi Joy

explained. "He lives here."

"Hi, Jay-Jay," I said. "I'm Sandi Daniels. That's my twin sister Randi."

"He knows all about you," Bobbi Joy interrupted. "I've told him lots about you two doofy dopes."

"Who's a doofy dope?" Randi snapped.

"You are," Bobbi snickered. "I still can't believe you fell for that trick. We heard you coming and hid. When I saw who it was, I couldn't believe it. I knew I could scare you guys since you don't know anything about the woods."

"We do too know something about the woods," replied Randi. I could tell she was getting upset. "Sandi's a G.L.O.W. Girl, and I know as much about the woods as you do!"

"Sure you do!" answered Bobbi Joy. "Next you'll be telling me that you can fish as well as I can. That's a laugh!"

Uh-oh! Of all the subjects for Bobbi Joy to bring up, that was the worst. She just had to mention fishing.

"I can out-fish you any day of the week!" Randi shouted. She was really riled up now. "I can out-fish you blindfolded! I can out-fish you with one hand tied behind my back!"

Bobbi Joy glanced at Jay-Jay. Then she looked back at Randi. "Do you want to bet on that?" she asked.

"Sure," replied Randi. "What's the bet?"

"I bet my partner and I catch more fish in the Lake Kickapoo junior fishing derby than you and your sister do," she said, smiling an evil smile. "The loser has to jump in the lake with her clothes on."

Randi glanced at me. I gritted my teeth and shook my head. "I already jumped in the lake with my clothes on, and I didn't like it," I whispered to Randi. "Leave me out of this."

Randi looked back at Bobbi Joy. "I guess there's no bet," Randi groaned.

"Are you chicken?" teased Bobbi Joy. It even made me angry when she started clucking like a chicken. "Are you afraid you'll lose?"

"I am not afraid," Randi snapped. "It's just that Sandi hates fishing."

"Okay then," proposed Bobbi Joy. "You can choose any partner you want."

Randi thought for a minute. I saw a faint smile on her lips. "Okay," she said. "It's a bet." Randi and Bobbi Joy shook hands.

"My partner will probably be a boy named Wormy Wormsley," Randi bragged to Bobbi. She had a big smile on her face, like she knew she had a secret weapon in the bet against Bobbi Joy.

"You and Nerdy Wormy!" shouted Bobbi Joy. "What a perfect couple!"

"Why? Do you know Wormy?" I asked.

"Sure!" Bobbi Joy replied. "Wormy is in Jay-Jay's class at school." She turned to her cousin. "Isn't that so, Jay-Jay?"

"Yup," Jay-Jay answered. "I know Wormy. I beat him in the fishing derby every year."

"Huh?" sputtered Randi. The smirk that

was on her face disappeared.

"By the way," Bobbi Joy began. "I think I forgot to tell you that Jay-Jay will be my partner for the bet." She laughed loudly.

"And I also forgot to tell you that Jay-Jay holds the record for the biggest fish ever caught in Lake Kickapoo."

Randi looked like she was turning green.

"Since the fishing derby lasts three days, the team that catches the most fish by combined weight over the three days wins," explained Bobbi Joy.

Randi nodded. What else could she do? Her temper had gotten her into another big mess.

"Good luck," Jay-Jay said to Randi as he and Bobbi started to walk away.

"So long!" Bobbi Joy yelled. "Watching you jump in the lake with your clothes on will be a real hoot." Her laughter echoed through the woods as Randi and I started back to our cabin.

"I'm a dead duck," Randi said as we walked along. "I don't have a chance."

"That's not true," I said. "You have a chance. I just hope Wormy will be your partner. Maybe you shouldn't have said he would do it without asking him first."

"I know," sighed Randi. "I just couldn't help myself. Bobbi Joy makes me so mad."

"Ranee! Sanee!" hollered Teddy when he spotted us.

Trouble came running toward us holding a big, plastic jar. "I catched a froggie!" he cried. "He my pet. His name is Hoppy."

Inside the jar was a huge, green, slimy bullfrog.

"Ick," I said. "Don't get that thing too close to me, Teddy."

"He's neat," Randi said.

"Hoppy is a great name," I told Teddy. "Just remember to keep him away from me."

"Hokay, Sanee," promised Trouble. "Sanee, don't worry about Hoppy."

Four

THE next morning started out with a bang—or maybe I should say a hop! When I rolled over in bed and opened my eyes, I saw two googly eyes staring back at me. First I thought it was just a bad dream and tried to fall back to sleep. But when I heard that awful sound, I knew my nightmare was real.

"RIBBET! RIBBET! CROAK!"

"EEEEK!" I screamed as my eyelids popped open and I sat up in bed. "Get that slimy thing out of my bed!" I yelled.

"RIBBET! CROAK!" Hoppy bounced off my covers and onto the cabin floor.

"What's the matter?" muttered Randi from her bed on the other side of the room.

"EEEK!" I screeched again as I pulled the bed covers up around my neck.

"Sandy? What's wrong?" Dad called from the hall. I heard steps down the hall. Dad, Mom, and Trouble came running into our room.

"Is it a snake? Or a mouse?" Mom asked. She had a frying pan in her hand. "We were just getting breakfast ready," she said.

Dad was dressed for his trip home on the train. And Teddy was still in his pajamas.

"Th-that thing was in my bed," I sputtered, pointing at the bullfrog squatting in the middle of the floor.

"Teddy!" Mom said. "How did that frog get in here?"

"Hoppy was code," Teddy said. "When I woke up I put him in Sanee's bed ta warm up my froggie," he explained.

Mom, Dad, and Randi burst out laughing. I didn't think it was so funny.

"Frogs always feel cold," Dad said to Teddy. "They're cold-blooded. From now on, keep

Hoppy in the jar in your room, or out he goes."

"Otay!" Teddy cried as he scooped Hoppy up in his hands. "I keep him in my room."

"Tell Sandi you're sorry," Mom said as she stopped Teddy at the door.

"Sorry, Sanee," said Trouble as he scooted away with his slimy, squirming frog.

"Well, anyway, I'm glad you're both awake now," Dad said. "It's time for breakfast. Mom has to drive me into town to catch the train pretty soon. So, please hurry and get dressed."

"Right, Dad," Randi said as she got out of bed and stumbled across the room. "We'll be dressed in a minute."

Mom and Dad went out and closed the door behind them. "What a way to wake up," I grumbled. "A frog is my alarm clock. Some vacation!"

"Stop complaining," Randi said. "It could be worse. Teddy could have put the tadpoles he caught in your water glass."

"Thanks for the warning," I answered.

"We'd better keep an eye on him."

At breakfast we all talked about what we were going to do all day. Mom had to drive Dad into town to catch the train for home. Randi was going fishing with Wormy. And me—I was going to pack a picnic lunch and spend a quiet day in the woods, taking notes for my wildlife speech.

But sometimes even the best plans can change. Maybe you noticed that the only person without any plans for the day was Teddy.

I thought Teddy would go with Mom. But Teddy didn't want to go for another ride in the car after yesterday's long trip. I really couldn't blame him. Teddy couldn't go fishing with Randi. I could just see Trouble in a canoe with Wormy and Randi. They'd need more than life jackets. They'd need life insurance. So, who did that leave? That's right—lucky me.

Actually, I didn't mind taking Teddy along on my walk through the woods. Teddy could be a little doll when he behaved. The question was—would he behave?

There was a knock at the cabin door just as Dad and I were finishing the dishes. It was Wormy.

"Good morning, Wormy," Dad said as he let Wormy in. "You're up early!"

"You have to get up early to hook the big ones," Wormy replied. He looked over at me and asked, "Are you ready to go, Randi?"

I smiled.

"Dat not Ranee!" Teddy cried. "Dat Sanee. Ranee in da libbing room."

"Huh?" asked Wormy as he stared at me.

I took my glasses out of my pocket and put them on.

"Oh," said Wormy, realizing his mistake. "I'm sorry, Sandi."

"Here I am, Wormy," Randi announced as she came out of the living room. "I'm all ready to go. I packed all my fishing gear last night. It's out on the porch."

39

Randi said good-bye to Dad, and then she left with Wormy. Then Mom and Dad got ready to go.

"Bye, Sandi," Dad said. "I'll be back to hear your wildlife speech at the end of the week." Teddy and I kissed Dad good-bye.

"Are you going to be okay here with Teddy? I'll be gone quite a while, Sandi," Mom said. "After I drop your father at the train station, I have to pick up some groceries in town."

"Don't worry," I said as we all walked out on the porch. "I'll take good care of Teddy." Teddy and I waved as the car drove off.

"Let's pack our lunch and get started on our nature hike," I said as I walked back into the house with Teddy.

"Can I bring Hoppy on da walk?" he asked.

"No way!" I said.

As I fixed our lunch, I told Teddy the story of Hansel and Gretel. Teddy listened quietly from start to finish. He loved the part about Hansel leaving a trail of crumbs to follow so they wouldn't get lost in the woods.

"Dat was a dood story," Teddy said when I finished.

I put my G.L.O.W. handbook, my nature note pad, and a pencil in the picnic basket along with our lunch. "We're ready to go," I announced. I took Teddy's hand, and we walked out of the cabin.

It was a beautiful day. First we strolled along the shore of Lake Kickapoo. Then we turned up a trail and followed a babbling brook into the woods. Every so often I stopped to jot down notes in my pad. Teddy and I saw plenty of animals. There were geese, ducks, and muskrats along the lake. Following the brook, we saw mice, turtles, and a roly-poly raccoon. In the woods we spotted a pheasant, a hawk, and a grumpy old groundhog who bolted down his hole when Teddy yelled, "What's dat?"

"That's a groundhog, Teddy," I explained.

In a clearing along the brook, we stopped for lunch. "I hungee," Teddy said as I opened the picnic basket. I handed Teddy his favorite food—a baloney sandwich. And, of course, his moze. I'd made tuna salad for myself.

"This has been a great nature walk," I said to Teddy as we munched. "I've got tons of notes for my speech."

"Tell me dat Hansel story again," pleaded Teddy as he chomped away on the middle of his sandwich. He hardly ever ate the crust.

"Well," I said, "okay. But only because you were so good on our walk and kept quiet when I asked you to."

The rest of our lunch break I spent telling the tale of Hansel and Gretel.

"Can I have nother boney sandwich?" Teddy asked when I finished the story.

"It's time to go," I replied

"I eat it on da way," Teddy replied.

"All right," I agreed. I unwrapped another sandwich for Teddy and handed it to him. I picked up the picnic basket. "Let's head for home, partner," I said and walked down the path with Teddy trailing behind me.

We'd walked quite a way before I realized what Teddy was doing with his sandwich. I turned around and caught him breaking off a bit of sandwich and tossing it behind us on the path.

"What are you doing?" I asked.

"I'm making a twail," Teddy explained. "Like Hansel did. I not wanna get lost."

"You're doing it backward," I tried to explain. "You're supposed to make the trail when you start a hike, not when you come back from one." When I reached out to take the sandwich, Teddy pulled away from me.

"I making a twail," he said. Rule number one with Teddy—don't argue with him.

"Okay, go ahead," I said. What harm could it do? We were almost back to the cabin, anyway. And making a food trail wasn't like littering.

Teddy kept leaving bits of bread and baloney behind us as we made our way from the lake to our cabin.

"Now are you happy, Hansel?" I asked when we got home.

"Yipes!" I yelled. I saw something waddling up the trail behind us, stopping here and there to nibble on Teddy's crumbs.

"Look!" cried Teddy when he finally noticed the black and white animal that was approaching us. "It's a kitty. A kitty-kat followed us home. Here kitty!"

"That's no kitty," I said as I picked up Teddy. "That's a skunk!"

We stood there and watched as the skunk ate his way toward us. Soon it would be right next to us! There was only one thing to do. Run!

Holding Teddy, I ran toward the cabin.

"Here Kitty! Kitty!" Trouble yelled as I ran with him. "Here Kitty!"

I opened the door and pushed Teddy inside. I jumped in and slammed the door behind me.

"You fraid of da kitty?" Teddy asked as he peered out the window. The skunk walked right up to the cabin. It was walking back and forth on the front porch. I bet it wanted more of Teddy's sandwich!

"I sure am afraid of it!" I said as I leaned back against the door to keep Teddy from opening it.

"Will da kitty go away?"

"I sure hope so," I replied. "And how many times do I have to tell you that's not a kitty? It's a skunk! And skunks stink! Boy, do they stink! Phew!"

"Phew?" said Teddy. "Lake Kickaphew. We lub you, Lake Kickaphew." Trouble sang as he ran around and around in a circle in the room.

"Kickaphew! Phew! Phew! Phew!"

Five

THE next day started off better than the day before had. At least I didn't wake up with a frog in my face. But breakfast seemed kind of lonely without Dad.

"Teddy, come away from the window, and eat your Super Pops," Mom said as we all sat down. Super Pops is Teddy's favorite cereal.

"He's been looking for that skunk ever since he woke up," Randi chuckled.

"Trouble still thinks it's a kitty," I said. "But don't remind me of yesterday. If Mom hadn't driven up in the car just then and frightened that skunk off the porch, I would have gone bonkers. Being locked up in a cabin alone with Teddy for three whole hours is not exactly a relaxing way to spend a vacation!"

I bit off a piece of toast and chewed it up. "Yesterday was the worst day of my life," I announced.

"It was a dood day," Teddy said, finally coming to the table.

"It was a good day for me, too," Randi said as she wolfed down her breakfast. I guess the mountain air made her extra hungry. Actually, everything made Randi extra hungry.

"I caught six fish," Randi continued. "And Wormy's going to be my partner for the fishing derby and the bet."

"Bet?" asked Mom. "What bet?"

"Uh-oh," Randi muttered as she glanced at me. We had told Mom and Dad about meeting up with Bobbi Joy Boikin, but we never mentioned Randi's bet.

"Bobbi Joy and Randi made a little bet on the fishing derby," I said.

"What kind of bet?" Mom asked. Randi sighed and spilled the beans about the bet.

She told Mom how she and Wormy would compete against Bobbi Joy and Jay-Jay. She also said that Wormy wanted to beat Jay-Jay as much as Randi wanted to beat Bobbi Joy. Randi kind of whispered the part about the loser having to jump in the lake with her clothes on.

Mom laughed and shook her head. "It sounds like a harmless enough bet," she said, with a glance at me. "Just make sure this competition between you and Bobbi Joy doesn't get out of hand. We don't want any double trouble at Lake Kickapoo."

"Kickaphew! Phew! Phew! Phew!" Teddy screeched.

"Be quiet, Teddy," Mom ordered.

Mom seemed worried about something, and I bet I knew what it was. Mom probably thought that Randi and I might try to pull one of our identity switching stunts on Bobbi Joy just to win the bet. Whenever Randi and I switch places, something bad always happened. Besides, how could switching identities help win a fishing derby?

"Don't worry, Mom," I said. "This bet has nothing to do with me. It's between Randi and Bobbi Joy."

After breakfast, Randi and I rode our bikes into town. Randi was meeting Wormy at the town hall to register for the fishing derby. I wanted to visit Ms. Morgan at the G.L.O.W. camp. Lucky for us, Mom said she would take Teddy for the morning.

It was a long ride around the lake, but a nice peaceful one. "Do you think you and Wormy have a chance against Bobbi Joy and Jay-Jay?" I asked Randi as we rode along into town.

"We'll beat them," Randi predicted. "Wormy and I make a great team. He's an expert on where to fish, and I'm an expert on which bait to use. Wormy likes to fish with worms, but I'm teaching him about lures and jigs."

"Uh, right, lures and jigs," I replied as we

rolled into the quiet town of Lakeview. I didn't want Randi to know I didn't have any idea what she was talking about. I didn't even know that there were types of artificial bait for catching fish.

Lakeview turned out to be a sleepy little town tucked away in the woods. At the end of the street we found the town hall. It was the biggest building in town. What made it even easier to spot was the fact that Wormy Wormsley was standing next to the front door.

"Hi, Randi. Hi, Sandi," said Wormy as we came to a stop.

"Hi, Wormy!" Randi shouted.

"Hello, Wormy," I said. "I hear you and Randi make a great fishing team."

"We sure do," Wormy replied. "I think I'm finally going to out-fish Jay-Jay Smith. He and I are friends, but I'd really like to beat him just once."

I nodded. "I think Randi would like to beat Bobbi Joy, too," I added.

"If we don't beat Bobbi Joy and Jay-Jay, I'll be taking a bath in the lake with my clothes on," Randi said as we started up the walk.

"Don't worry," Wormy said. "It's Bobbi Joy who'll be taking the bath."

"Oh, yeah? What's that supposed to mean?" someone yelled. We stopped at the entrance to the building. Bobbi and Jay-Jay walked out.

"I didn't mean anything, Bobbi Joy," Wormy apologized.

"Yeah," said Bobbi Joy. "We'll see who gets to take the bath. I have a feeling that Jay-Jay and I are going to win this derby by a mile."

She gave a loud laugh. It was a laugh I had heard back home a hundred times.

Jay-Jay said, "Hey, Bobbi Joy, let's go. We have to go home and work on our fishing rods, to make sure they're in good shape for the derby."

"If our main competition is these two doofs," Bobbi Joy boasted, "I don't think our rods have to be in good shape. We could beat

these guys with bamboo poles and marshmallows for bait."

"Aw, knock it off," said Jay-Jay. "I don't want all your big talk to backfire on us."

Then he turned to us and said, "Seriously, good luck, you guys. I know we're the two best teams, and one of us will win."

Bobbi Joy frowned, and Jay-Jay smiled. Then they left.

I just shook my head. "How can such a nice guy be related to Bobbi Joy?" I asked.

"Hey, wait a minute," Randi said, staring at me. "It's against the rules to have a crush on the enemy."

"Randi!" I screamed. "I don't have a crush on Jay-Jay. I don't even know him."

"Right," Randi said and smiled a funny smile. "You don't even know him. How could I ever think you had a crush on him?"

"Let's go inside, Randi," said Wormy. "We have to go sign up for the derby."

Six

"WELL, we're all signed up," announced Wormy when they came out of the town hall.

"Yeah," said Randi. "All we have to do now is win the darn contest." Then Randi said, "Hey, Wormy, Sandi wants to stop at the G.L.O.W. camp before we head for home. Can you tell us the easiest way to get there?"

"I'll ride along and show you the way," he offered.

After about a half an hour, we came to the gate of the camp. It was almost directly across the lake from our cabin. Wormy pointed it out to us and cycled off with a wave.

"See you on Wednesday, partner!" he

shouted to Randi.

Randi and I rode up a dirt road into the G.L.O.W. camp. Soon we saw a bunch of log cabins and buildings, but we didn't see any people. I remembered the campers hadn't arrived yet. They were still getting the camp ready. We went into one building and asked a woman in a G.L.O.W. uniform if she knew where Ms. Morgan was.

"I'm Ms. Abigail Crump. Ms. Morgan is in the meeting hall," said the woman. "My, my, you two girls look alike," she added with a laugh. "I don't think I could tell you apart if not for your glasses," she said, pointing at me.

We just smiled and walked away.

Randi and I walked over to the meeting hall and found Ms. Morgan. She was glad to see us. After we talked for a while about Lake Kickapoo and the G.L.O.W. camp, Ms. Morgan said she would like me to give my speech on Friday.

"By then, all the G.L.O.W. girls will be here,"

she said. "Will 2:00 be okay?"

"That's great," I answered. "I really hope I get this merit badge," I added.

"I'm sure you'll do just fine, Sandi," Ms. Morgan said. "I'll pick you up at 1:00, so your mom doesn't have to drive you over here."

It was all settled. I was feeling super about having the chance to give my speech and getting my merit badge.

"Bye," said Randi as we went out the door and got on our bikes and headed for home.

Randi and I didn't talk much as we rode back to our cabin. We both had a lot on our minds. I was thinking about my speech and about earning my merit badge. Randi was probably thinking about the big fishing derby. We both knew that an exciting week was ahead.

We didn't realize that the excitement was going to begin a little early.

Seven

"LOOK!" shouted Randi as we rode up to the clearing in front of our cabin. "Do you see what I see?"

"Yes!" I gulped. "It's that skunk again! Thanks to Teddy, it's still hanging around the cabin."

"Should we stop?" Randi asked as she slowed her bicycle and coasted. "Should we turn around?"

"It's too late for that," I answered. "It sees us. And it's headed right at us. I guess it thinks we have food."

"What should we do, Miss Wildlife?"

"Yell!" I shouted. "Holler at the top of your lungs. Maybe we can scare him away."

"Right," said Randi.

"EEEK!" We shrieked and waved our arms. "YEOW! EEEEYOUU! ARRGH!" We sounded like two wild goblins.

I'm sure that poor skunk had never heard anything like the Daniels twins' alarm sirens. The terrified little thing scampered off into the bushes.

"What on earth is going on out here?" Mom cried as she opened the cabin door and stormed out onto the porch.

Randi and I coasted to a stop by her. "That skunk was out here again," Randi said. "We had to scare it away."

"You sure scared me to death," Mom said. Then she whispered, "Don't tell Teddy about the skunk. If he finds out that the skunk is still around, he'll go looking for it."

"We won't tell him," Randi promised. "I just hope that's the last we see of that skunk."

I shook my head. "I think that skunk is here to stay—thanks to Trouble."

The rest of that day and the next day zoomed by. I spent Tuesday morning arranging my notes into a 30-minute speech on the wildlife of Lake Kickapoo. Tuesday afternoon, I began memorizing the speech. It didn't take long. My speech was full of interesting information. I even threw in a joke about finding Teddy's pet frog in my bed. I said that I almost croaked from the shock. Ha-ha!

The days went fast for Randi, too. She spent most of the time getting ready for the fishing derby. She and Teddy dug up worms to use as bait just in case the lures and jigs didn't work. Teddy loved digging up the worms!

Tuesday night after dinner, I tested my speech on Mom and Randi and Teddy. Teddy interrupted about a million times. He kept getting up to check the worms he and Randi had left in an old can on the porch.

After I finished giving my speech for them, Randi announced she was turning in early. "The fishing derby starts tomorrow. Wormy and I want to get an early start."

"Good night, Randi," I said as I put my speech notes into the briefcase I'd brought along from home. It was Dad's old one.

Randi went into our bedroom and closed the door.

A few minutes later, a piercing shriek echoed from our bedroom. Mom and I jumped. Teddy came running in from the porch. Randi threw open the door to our room and stormed out holding Hoppy in her hands.

"This darn frog was under my pillow!" she yelled.

"Teddy," said Mom, "I told you to keep Hoppy out of your sisters' room."

"I sorry," said Teddy, taking Hoppy from Randi. "I losed him."

"Keep that thing away from me...or...or I'll use him for bait!" Randi warned as she turned and stomped back into the bedroom. She slammed the door behind her.

I closed my briefcase. "You'd better keep

Hoppy in a safe place, Teddy," I said.

"Safe place?" he repeated.

"Yes," I explained. "Keep Hoppy in a safe place like I do with my notes for my speech. I don't want to lose them, so I keep them in my briefcase." I tapped on the lid of the closed briefcase. "If you want Hoppy to be safe, keep him in a safe place. Do you understand?"

"I unnerstan," Teddy answered.

"Good," I said.

The next morning we were all up bright and early. Randi had her fishing gear ready when Wormy knocked at the door.

"Good morning everyone," Wormy said when Mom opened the door. "Are you ready to go, Randi? To catch the big ones, you've got to get out early."

"I'm all set," Randi said as she collected her gear and moved toward the door.

"Good luck, you guys!" we all shouted as they were leaving. "Good fishing!"

The morning of the first day of the derby

passed quickly. I studied my speech and helped Mom straighten up the cabin. After four and a half days, the place was a bit messy. Around 1:00, I decided to make a pitcher of lemonade for when Randi and Wormy returned. That's when I found Teddy had stored about a dozen tadpoles in our lemonade pitcher.

"MOM!" I yelled. "Look what Trouble did," I said pointing at the tadpoles in the water-filled pitcher.

Teddy was taking a nap at the time, lucky for him. Mom wasn't angry at all. Maybe it was because he looks so cute when he's asleep. Don't be fooled by him, I wanted to tell Mom.

"Just take the tadpoles down to the lake and dump them out," Mom said. She's pretty understanding sometimes.

I had just dumped out the tadpoles when I saw Wormy and Randi floating up in the canoe.

"How did you do?" I shouted.

"We were great!" Randi yelled back. "Wormy hooked a four-pound bass."

The canoe touched the beach, and I helped pull it in.

"All in all, we caught almost 10 pounds of fish," Wormy said.

"Wow!" I said. "Welcome back, champs!" I shouted.

Wormy laughed. "I don't know about champs, but it's a good start," he said.

"The best part is we beat Bobbi Joy and Jay-Jay," Randi continued. "Jay-Jay caught some fair-size fish, but Bobbi Joy caught zilch!"

"We're ahead of them by several pounds," Wormy said as we started up the path.

"It looks like the bet is in the bag," Randi bragged. "And pretty soon Bobbi Joy will be in the lake!"

"I'll make some fresh lemonade," I said.

"I have a feeling that tomorrow we'll do even better!" Randi predicted.

Well, Randi knows a lot about fishing, but she stinks as a fortune teller. Her prediction was way off. On Thursday, Wormy caught a few medium-size fish. But all Randi managed to hook were a few fish the size of Teddy's tadpoles!

And to make things worse, Jay-Jay and Bobbi Joy had a great day. Jay-Jay hooked a whopper that was almost as big as the record-setting fish he'd caught a year ago. And Bobbi Joy caught several big ones, too. So, they took the lead.

On Thursday night, Randi, Wormy, and I were sitting on our front porch. Randi was telling me how Bobbi Joy was teasing her at the weigh-in.

"Bobbi Joy was really getting on my nerves," Randi said, gritting her teeth.

"Don't get so upset," I said. "You haven't lost yet. Tomorrow is another day."

"That's right," Wormy agreed. "They're only ahead of us by two pounds of fish. That's the

67

closest I've ever been to Jay-Jay in a tournament. Usually, I'm way, way behind, but this time I've actually got a great chance of winning."

"I guess you really want to win, don't you?" I asked Wormy.

"It would be nice to win," he answered. "Jay-Jay's all right, but he always wins. I'd like to see him lose just once."

"Do you actually think we have a chance?" Randi asked Wormy.

"Sure we do," Wormy said. "And Bobbi Joy thinks we have a chance, too."

"How do you know that?" Randi asked.

"Well, didn't you see her face at the weigh-in when I told you I know a super-secret fishing spot?" Wormy asked. "Take my word for it—Bobbi Joy is worried about the last day of the derby."

Randi's face brightened. She actually smiled. "Yeah, you're right, Wormy," she admitted. "Bobbi Joy did look worried. I bet she'd do anything to find out where your secret spot is."

"Is your secret spot that good?" I asked. Wormy nodded. "Yeah. It's a deep hole where a creek runs into the lake," he said. "There are some really humongous fish down there. Of course, I've never caught any of them."

"Just wait until tomorrow," Randi said.

"Wait a minute, Randi," I said. "Don't count your chickens before they're hatched. Or, don't count your fish before they're hooked. A lot of things could happen tomorrow."

"Like what?" asked Randi.

I shrugged. "Well, I don't know," I said. "Something could happen. Anything could happen."

"Who wants popcorn?" shouted Mom from inside the cabin.

"We do!" we all yelled and raced inside.

Eight

MY big day finally arrived.

T.G.I.F.—Thank Goodness It's Friday! That's what I kept thinking over and over as I spread out my G.L.O.W. Girl uniform on my bed. I had the room all to myself. In fact, I had the cabin all to myself. Mom had taken Teddy for a walk, and Randi was outside on the porch waiting for Wormy.

Everything was quiet and peaceful. And I really felt super. I was ready to give my speech. I was sure nothing could go wrong. I was sure I'd get the merit badge I'd dreamed of for so long. Today was the day Sandi Daniels had waited for since vacation began. It was my day!

I looked around for my briefcase. I really

didn't need the notes because I knew my speech by heart. But I wanted to have them, just in case.

"Where is that briefcase? It was right here," I said out loud as I searched our bedroom, the living room, and the kitchen. It wasn't anywhere.

I went out onto the porch. Randi was sitting at the top of the stairs messing around with her fishing gear.

"Have you seen my briefcase?" I asked her.

"Teddy had it earlier," she said. "He was fooling around with it. I bet it's in his room."

"I bet it is, too," I grumbled. "Trouble just can't keep his hands off other people's stuff." I took off my glasses. I pulled a tissue out of my pocket and cleaned the lenses.

"Are you going to wear glasses or contacts for your speech?" Randi asked.

"I'm going to wear my contacts," I replied. "My glasses slip down my nose when I bow my head."

Randi nodded. "Good luck today," she said. "I'll be back in plenty of time to hear your speech."

"Good luck to you, too," I said. "But you probably won't need luck if you fish at Wormy's secret spot," I added. "Where is it again?"

Just then we heard a rustling in the bushes near the side of the house. It sounded like someone was hiding in there, maybe trying to hear what we were saying.

"What's that?" I whispered to Randi.

Randi made a sour face. "I bet I know who that is," Randi whispered. "Bobbi Joy would do anything to find out where Wormy's secret spot is."

I nodded. I remembered how Bobbi Joy had hidden in the bushes and scared us on our first day at the lake.

"Keep talking," Randi whispered. "I'm going to teach that sneak a lesson she won't forget."

"Hey, Randi," I began in a loud voice. "Didn't Wormy say the biggest fish in the lake are in that secret spot." As I was talking, Randi tiptoed down the stairs and sneaked around the back of the bushes.

"Now I've got you!" Randi yelled as she jumped into the bushes. "Come out of there, Bobbi Joy!"

The next thing I heard was a squeal. Then Randi screamed! After that I didn't hear anything else. But I smelled something. And it smelled terrible!

Bobbi Joy Boikin didn't come out of the bushes. What did waddle out of the bushes was the skunk that had followed Teddy home. It scooted past the porch and ran off into the woods. Finally, Randi came out.

"UGH!" groaned Randi as she stood there with her arms stretched out like a scarecrow.

"P.U.!" I yelled holding my nose. "You smell awful!"

"Thanks for telling me, Sandi," she said sarcastically. "That miserable skunk sprayed me! What a way to start the day. Nothing could be

worse than this."

"Don't be too sure about that," I gasped, backing further away. "Look out there!" I pointed down at the lake. From the porch I could see a canoe on the lake making for our shore. It was Wormy.

"Oh, no!" groaned Randi. "I can't let him see me like this!"

"You mean, smell you like that," I said. "Do you have a choice?"

"Help me!" begged Randi as she paced back and forth, leaving a terrible smell wherever she went. "Think of something. Do something. Help me out of this smelly mess," she pleaded.

"I could meet Wormy at the water's edge and tell him you're sick or something," I suggested.

"I can't be sick," Randi told me. "I have to be at the derby check-in, or our team will be disqualified. I can't let Wormy down now. I can't go fishing with him, but I have to go. What am I going to do?"

Poor Randi was frantic. And time was running out fast. Wormy's canoe was getting closer and closer to shore. "You're the smart twin," she said to me. "Think!" Randi begged. "How can I be in two places at once?"

Just then Randi stopped pacing. She froze in her tracks. Slowly she turned toward me. She looked at me in a strange way. It was a look I had seen before.

"Oh, no," I sputtered shaking my head. "I know what you're thinking. We can't do it. I can't do it. I won't pretend to be you. I won't!"

"Why not?" Randi shouted. "It's my only hope. We've done it before."

"Oh, right," I said. "Don't you remember? We've ended up in trouble each time!"

"This time will be different," Randi promised. "No one will ever know. What can go wrong if you go fishing with Wormy in my place?"

"A lot can go wrong," I answered. "Besides, I hate fishing. And what about giving my nature speech this afternoon at 2:00?"

"You can fake the fishing end of it," Randi said. "Just let Wormy catch all the fish. And you'll be back way before Ms. Morgan shows up to drive you into town. I already told Wormy I have to return early. You've got to help me, Sandi."

I pinched my nose closed again and shook my head. "Nope. No way! Absolutely not."

"Thanks a whole lot," Randi said with a sigh. "I guess Bobbi Joy will win our bet then. And Wormy will be disappointed. And your sister is going to be the laughing stock of the world when Bobbi Joy tells everyone I had to drop out of the contest because I got sprayed by a skunk. I'll be embarrassed to death. My life is over!"

What could I do? I didn't want Randi to be a laughing stock. I didn't want her to have to disappoint Wormy. I didn't want Bobbi Joy to win the bet and go around making fun of us. We Daniels had to stick together, didn't we?

And maybe no one would ever know if we pulled the old switcheroo at Lake Kickapoo. The plan seemed foolproof.

"Okay," I agreed with a sigh. "I'll do it."

"Hooray!" cheered my smelly sister, jumping up and down. Her jumping around actually made the smell worse, so I told her to calm down.

"Quick!" Randi ordered like an army general. "Go change into some of my clothes. Put your contact lenses on. Then grab my fishing gear, and get down to the lake to meet Wormy. I don't want him to come up here."

"Right," I called as I dashed back into the cabin. I ran into our room. I removed my glasses and put in my contacts. I tore off my clothes and dressed in a pair of Randi's jeans and one of her Washington Redskins football jerseys.

"Grab my fishing gear!" Randi shouted. "Hurry. He's almost to shore."

"Okay! Okay! Just don't come any closer,"

I warned. "That smell is making me sick." I picked up the gear. "Look in my G.L.O.W. Girl handbook while I'm gone," I said. "It'll tell you how to get rid of that smell."

"Fine. Now, get going!" yelled Randi. "Hurry. And thanks!"

I waved to Randi and rushed off toward the path that led down to the water's edge. There was no time to spare. Wormy's canoe was almost to shore.

Nine

"Randi, what are you doing down here?" Wormy called as he beached his canoe. *Good. He doesn't know who I really am.*

"Uh, I came down so we could get an early start," I explained as I hopped into the front of the canoe and put on my life jacket.

Wormy probably noticed how nervous I was because he said, "You're acting kind of funny. Is everything okay?"

"I'm just a little nervous about the last day of the derby," I answered.

Wormy sniffed the air. "Phew," he groaned. "It smells like that skunk has been around again and something scared it away."

"Something scared it, all right," I mumbled

as I fastened my life jacket.

"Huh?"

"Umm, I said I'm scared that we won't do well today," I said. "Especially since we have to weigh in early."

"Don't worry. I didn't forget about Sandi's speech," Wormy answered. "We'll be back in plenty of time. I want to hear it, too. I bet it's going to be great."

I smiled.

Wormy looked at my face. "Are you sure everything is okay?" he asked again. "There's something different about you, but I don't know exactly what it is."

"Oh, I'm just a little tired," I answered. "I didn't sleep very well last night. I was, umm, worried about the fishing derby." Then I thought I'd better change the subject. "Shouldn't we be getting to the check-in?" I asked.

"Yeah, you're right," said Wormy as he started to back paddle. "Shove us off, Randi."

I nodded. I picked up my paddle and pushed off. Wormy paddled some more to move us backward, and then he turned the canoe. He started to paddle across the lake toward the check-in spot.

I didn't do anything. I'd never been that far out in water in a canoe before. It was wobbly and scary. It felt like we would tip over any minute. I sat frozen to my seat with my hands clamped on the sides of the canoe.

"Aren't you going to paddle?" Wormy asked.

"N-not today," I sputtered. "I-I want to save my energy for fishing."

"Okay," said Wormy. "I'll do the paddling."

Boy was I glad when we reached the other side of the lake. My knees were knocking as we climbed out of the canoe. Lucky for me, Wormy didn't notice.

"I'll check in at the judges' stand," Wormy said as he left me standing by the canoe. As soon as he was gone, Jay-Jay and Bobbi Joy walked up to me.

"Hi, guys," I said.

"Hi, Randi," answered Jay-Jay. "Good luck today. You and Wormy are giving us a real fight."

"Yeah! Good luck, nerd," Bobbi Joy said. "Even if you go to Wormy's secret spot, you'll need lots of luck to catch any fish."

Just then Bobbi Joy stopped talking and looked at me in a funny way. I didn't like the way she kept staring at me. Did she suspect anything? I had to say something that would make her think I was Randi.

"Get outta my face, Bobbi Joy!" I shouted. That seemed to work.

"I can't wait to see you jump in the lake, Randi Daniels," Bobbi Joy grumbled as she walked off.

"Say hi to Sandi for me," Jay-Jay said. "I hear she's giving a speech at the G.L.O.W. Girl camp today. Maybe I'll go to it." Jay-Jay blushed a little. He seemed embarrassed.

"I'm sure Sandi would like to see you there,"

I replied. Hmm, if it wasn't for Bobbi Joy and that skunk, this would be our best vacation ever.

"Are you ready, Randi?" Wormy asked as he walked up. "We're all checked in. Now it's time to fish."

"Hey, Wormy," said Jay-Jay. "Good luck."

"The same to you," Wormy replied. The boys shook hands.

Wormy and I got back into the canoe. We shoved off and paddled out on the lake. Wormy paddled, that is. I just held on for dear life and "saved my energy" for fishing.

"There's my secret spot," Wormy said after we crossed the lake. He pointed to a small cove that had thick bushes growing along the water's edge. Only a tiny strip of beach was visible.

"Do you want to fish from the canoe or from shore?" Wormy asked.

"Let's fish from shore...if you don't mind," I replied. I would have done anything to get out of that boat.

"You sure are acting strange today," said Wormy as we neared the narrow strip of shore. "All the other times you wanted to fish from the canoe."

"I just need a change today," I replied.

Wormy nodded and beached the canoe. We climbed out and took off our life jackets. The cove did look like a good place to fish. A wide brook emptied into the lake near big clumps of wild berry bushes. Birds were everywhere, too. There were lots of nests in the bushes. Actually, I didn't care that much about the fish or the birds. I was just glad to have my feet on solid ground again.

"Here's your pole," said Wormy as he handed me Randi's rod.

"Thanks," I said as I took the pole.

"What are you going to use for bait?" Wormy asked. "Are you going to use a jig or a lure?"

"Oh, I don't know," I replied. I had no idea what bait to use. "What are you going to use?"

"I thought I'd try some of these for a change," he said. He took a small cardboard box out of his tackle box. He opened the cardboard box.

"UGH!" I groaned as I looked inside. There were live crickets in the box. Wormy picked up a cricket and held it between his fingers.

"Do you want one? The bass snap them up."

"No way!" I shrieked, shuddering from head to toe.

Wormy stared at me in astonishment.

"What I mean, uh," I said, "is that crickets aren't good bait this early in the day."

"Oh," replied Wormy. He seemed totally convinced that I knew what I was talking about. He put the cricket back in the box and closed the lid. Then he picked up a can and held it out toward me. "How about one of these?"

I gagged. The can was full of squirmy, wiggly worms.

"Are you sure you're okay?" asked Wormy as he plucked a worm out of the can.

"I-I'm fine," I lied as I watched Wormy stick the worm on his hook. "I just want to test some new bait I thought up."

"New bait?" asked Wormy. "Can I see it?"

"No! Not yet," I stalled. "I want to make sure it works first."

"Okay," said Wormy. "You fish here by the creek. I'll try down the beach."

Wormy took his tackle box and walked away. He glanced back at me like I was acting weird. And I was. I was almost tempted to tell him who I really was. But I knew if I told him, he'd get really angry because we'd tricked him. I decided to just fish and keep my mouth shut.

But how could I fish? What could I use for bait? There was no way I was going to stick a bug or a worm on my hook. That was just too gross! I couldn't ask Wormy to bait my hook. Then he'd know for sure I wasn't Randi. Using one of Randi's lures or jigs was out, too.

I didn't really know anything about them. And if I fished with a bare hook, Wormy would find out for sure what a fake I was. I didn't know what to do.

I walked toward the place where the creek emptied into the lake. I passed huge sticker bushes with big black berries on them. "Hmm," I said. "Maybe I can use a berry for bait."

I walked up to a bush. On one of the branches I saw a downy white feather stuck on a thorn. "I'll use that, too," I said.

I picked a big juicy berry and snatched the feather out of the bush. Carefully I pushed the berry onto the hook. Then I pushed the quill part of the tiny feather through the tip of the hook. It stuck fine.

"There's my bait," I said. "Nothing in the world will be attracted to this," I told myself.

I tossed the hook into the water. It landed with a loud splash. I smiled and sat down on the beach to wait. I wasn't waiting for a bite.

I was just waiting for time to pass. I thought about my speech. I wanted the hours to go fast.

But time didn't go fast. The minutes crept by. The fish didn't bite. The sun got hot. The water got warm. Wormy tried every kind of bait he could think of. Nothing worked. He moved up and down the lake front. That didn't help, either. He never got a nibble.

And me? The last thing I wanted was a nibble, because then I'd have to touch some slimy fish.

"Do you want to move to another spot?" I yelled to Wormy after we'd been there for a long time.

"I guess we'd better try a new place," said Wormy with a sigh. "I can't believe my secret spot let us down."

"Okay," I said. "Then I might as well reel in." I stood up and started to take in my line.

Then it happened! Something pulled on my line so hard it almost jerked the pole right out of my hands.

"Whoa!" I yelled as I tried to hold on to the bending, shaking, and jiggling pole. "I-I've got something! Wormy, come quick!"

"Holy flying flounder!" shouted Wormy as he dropped his pole and ran toward me. "Hang on! Whatever you do, don't let go."

"I'll try not to," I said as I leaned back and held onto the rod with all my strength.

Wormy reached my side and grabbed the pole. I couldn't have held on much longer.

"Reel it in, Randi!" shouted Wormy. "Reel as fast as you can."

I started to crank the reel. Together Wormy and I pulled.

"It feels like a sea monster," I said.

KA-SPLASH! Out of the lake leaped a huge silver fish. KA-SPLASH! Back into the water it went.

"It's a whopper of a lake trout!" Wormy yelled. "It's the biggest one I've ever seen. Pull, Randi! Pull!"

Even though I've never liked fishing, it was pretty awesome fighting that big fish.

"There! Now we've got him!" Wormy shouted as we pulled the big fish out of the water and up onto shore. It wiggled and flopped around.

"Wow!" I said as I stared at my catch. I couldn't believe my eyes. "That's some fish."

"It's a record fish, for sure," said Wormy. "It's bigger than the one Jay-Jay caught two years ago. You must have used some super bait to hook him."

"I did," I said. "But now what do we do?"

"We take him to get weighed," Wormy said.

"But won't he die if we keep him out of the water?" I asked. The thought of my fish dying made me sad. "I don't want to kill him," I told Wormy. "If he'll die going to the weigh-in, let's throw him back right now."

"What?" cried Wormy. "This fish is sure to win the derby for us. You're joking."

"No, I'm not," I answered. "Isn't there a way

to keep the fish alive so we can throw him back after the weigh-in?"

Wormy thought for a minute. "We could put him on a stringer and keep him in the water for now," said Wormy. "Then I could paddle home while you wait here. I have a big ice chest at home. I could bring it back. We could fill it with water and put the fish in there."

"That sounds good," I said. "Get going."

"It's going to take a while," said Wormy. I shrugged my shoulders. "That doesn't matter," I said. "The most important thing is keeping the fish alive. Put him on that stringer thing, and go get that chest. I'll wait here until you get back."

"Okay, Randi, I'll do it," said Wormy. "But since when did you get so tender-hearted about a fish?"

I just looked at him without answering.

Ten

I worried about that poor fish the whole time Wormy was gone.

"Thank goodness you're back!" I shouted when Wormy finally came back.

"We have to hurry," Wormy said. "Or, we won't make the weigh-in." He quickly filled the ice chest with water and put the fish in it. The fish splashed in the water.

"Will it be all right?" I asked as I put on my life jacket.

"It'll be fine," Wormy answered. "We're sure going to get a lot of attention for this fish."

We put our gear in the canoe and hopped in. Wormy paddled so fast I had to hold on to the canoe extra tight.

As we got near the weigh-in area, Bobbi Joy and Jay-Jay were waiting on the shore.

"Did you catch anything?" Jay-Jay shouted to Wormy.

"Nope," replied Wormy. "I didn't catch a thing. How about you?"

"I didn't even get a nibble!" Jay-Jay yelled back. "None of the teams caught much today. It was just too hot. Bobbi Joy landed the biggest catch of the day. She hooked a two-pound bass."

"That means we're going to win the derby—and the bet," Bobbi Joy called out to me. She grinned from ear to ear.

"Don't be too sure about that," Wormy said with a laugh. "I said *I* didn't catch anything. Randi hooked a sea monster!"

"WHAT!" screamed Bobbi Joy as our canoe slid onto the shore. She and Jay-Jay came running over to our boat and looked at the fish in the chest.

"Holy halibut!" yelled Jay-Jay when he saw

the lake trout splashing around in the water. He turned toward the crowd at the weigh-in stand. "Hey, everybody!" he hollered. "Come over here and check out this whopper!"

Wormy and I got out of the boat. Wormy grinned from ear to ear. I just stood there. I didn't know what to do or say.

"Why is the fish in that ice chest?" Bobbi Joy asked.

Before I could speak, Wormy answered for me. "Randi didn't want to kill the fish," he explained. "She wants to throw it back into the lake after it's weighed. She's sentimental about it."

Bobbi Joy glared at me. "Sentimental?" she muttered. "Randi Daniels is not the sentimental type. There's something fishy going on here."

Luckily, a crowd gathered around us just then. They started to talk, so I didn't have to face Bobbi Joy.

"It's a whopper!" whistled one judge.

"If that's not a new record fish, I'll eat my life jacket," said another judge.

"Let's weigh that monster," said a third judge.

The judges lifted the wiggling fish out of the chest and carried it to the weighing stand.

"Be careful," I said. "I want to throw it back after it's weighed."

A newspaper reporter who was covering the final day of the derby came up to me. "Did I hear you right?" he asked me. "Did you say you're going to turn that fish loose?"

"Yes, sir," I replied.

"Now that's a story!" he cried. "Her fish is the biggest one ever caught in Lake Kickapoo. It's bigger than the one Jay-Jay Smith caught two years ago. And she's going to throw it back!"

"And here's another story!" shouted a judge. "Those two kids win the junior derby. It's official!" He handed me and Wormy a nice trophy.

"Hooray!" cried Wormy as he jumped up and down.

"Congratulations, Randi," said Jay-Jay as he shook hands with me. He really was a good sport. Losing the contest and having his record broken didn't seem to bother him.

"Now, miss, I'd like to ask you a few questions," said the newspaper man. "What did you use for bait?"

I looked at Wormy and winked. "I'm sorry, but that's a secret," I said.

The newspaper man laughed. "Okay," he said. "What's your name?" he asked.

I gulped! My name? Oh, no! How could I tell him my name? I wasn't me. I was supposed to be Randi. There was a long pause as everyone waited for me to tell him my name. Bobbi Joy was staring at me hard.

"Uh," I said.

"Her name is Randi Daniels," Wormy finally said ending the long silence. "And I'm Walter Warren Wormsley III, her partner."

"Let's get a picture of Randi and Walter with their trophy," the reporter called to his photographer. "And then let's get a picture of them with her fish before she puts it back in the lake." The reporter smiled at me. "Step over here, Randi."

"Yeah!" yelled Bobbi Joy. "Step over there— Randi!" The way she said it made me plenty nervous. Had she guessed the truth?

The interviews, photographs, and questions seemed to last forever. Finally, it was time to turn the fish loose. Wormy and I dumped the lake trout out of the ice chest and into the water. He splashed in the shallow water for a few seconds. Then he darted off into the middle of the lake. Turning the fish loose made me feel happy.

"Good-bye, fish," I said. "Thanks for helping us win the derby."

"Well, maybe we'd better get going," said Wormy. "It's getting late."

"Oh my gosh!" I yelled. In all the excitement

I'd forgotten about the time. "What time is it?" I shouted frantically.

"It's 1:15," somebody said.

"I have to get home!" I screamed, running for Wormy's canoe.

"Randi, calm down!" shouted Wormy as he raced after me. "Sandi won't mind if we're a little late. She'll understand."

"Sandi *will* mind," I babbled as I strapped on my life jacket. "She *won't* understand. Hurry."

I hopped in the canoe. Wormy jumped in after me. He put our trophy in the boat and pushed off. I picked up a paddle. There was no time to be afraid now. I had to get across the lake fast. "Paddle! Paddle quickly!" I shouted.

"Okay! Okay!" Wormy answered as the boat began to glide through the water. "I said it before, and I'll say it again," Wormy puffed. "You sure are acting strange today, Randi."

Eleven

AS soon as the canoe touched the other side, I hopped out and raced up the path toward the cabin.

"Hey! Wait for me!" yelled Wormy. But I couldn't wait. I was already out of time and in big trouble.

"Phew!" I groaned when I reached the front of the cabin. The place still smelled of skunk. I wrinkled up my nose and looked around. The car was gone. I guessed that Mom and Teddy had left already to go pick up Dad. I ran up the porch steps and burst through the cabin door.

"Randi?" I shouted. "Randi! Are you here?"

No one answered. The place was empty.

"Where is she?" I cried as I bolted into our

bedroom. I stopped in the middle of our room and looked at my bed.

"Uh-oh," I groaned. My G.L.O.W. Girl uniform was gone. So were my glasses. On the dresser where my glasses used to be was a slip of paper that looked like a note.

"Oh, no," I gulped as I walked toward the dresser. "Randi didn't, did she?"

I picked up the note.

Sandi,

Where are you? I looked in your G.L.O.W. Girl handbook and found a way to get rid of the skunk smell. Mom and Teddy went into town to pick up Dad. They're going to have lunch together and then go right to the G.L.O.W. Girl camp. I was supposed to go with you. Mom doesn't know anything about what's going on.

I was hoping you would be back before Ms. Morgan arrived. But you weren't! When she came to pick you up, I panicked. I know how much that merit badge means to you.

So, since you are being me, I decided to be you. I went with Ms. Morgan. She didn't suspect a thing. Hurry over to the camp. You know how much I hate speaking to a crowd. I'll stall as long as I can.

Randi

P.S. I found your briefcase in Teddy's room. I took the notes with me in case I have to give your speech. But I hope I don't! Please hurry!

I heard a knock at the open cabin door. "Can I come in?" Wormy called.

I put down Randi's note. "Come on in, Wormy," I called. I walked out to the living room.

"I have to tell you something, and I hope you won't be angry," I said.

"Why would I be angry?" muttered Wormy.

"How could anything make me angry today? Wormy Wormsley and Randi Daniels just won the fishing derby."

"Well, that's the problem. I'm not Randi."

"Huh?" sputtered Wormy.

"I'm Sandi," I replied. "Randi got sprayed by a skunk this morning and couldn't go fishing. So, I took her place."

"Holy pickled perch!" Wormy exclaimed. "I knew there was something different about you, Randi. I mean, Sandi," he corrected. "Where's the real Randi now?"

"She's in big trouble," I said. "She's at the G.L.O.W. Girl camp pretending to me be. And if we don't get over there fast, she's going to have to give my merit badge speech."

"Holy jumping catfish!" Wormy cried. "Come on, We've got to help Randi. Let's get back to the canoe. Cutting across the lake is the fastest way to get to the camp."

We rushed out of the cabin. I glanced at the clock on the mantle. It was already 1:45.

My speech was due to begin right at 2:00. I wondered if we would make it in time.

We paddled as hard as we could, but I didn't know if it would be hard enough.

"It's not much further," said Wormy. We were both out of breath. "After today, I'm not getting in this canoe again for a while," he added.

The canoe touched the shore just outside of the G.L.O.W. Girl camp. We hopped out, stowed our paddles and life jackets in the boat, and ran up toward the meeting hall.

"I hope we're not too late," I said. As we came out of the woods near the buildings, we spotted lots of cars parked in front of the meeting hall. "There's our car," I pointed out. "Mom and Dad and Teddy are here already."

Wormy looked around. "There's nobody out here," he said. "Everyone must be inside."

"Let's look in there," I said, pointing and walking toward a window. "Maybe I can find a way to switch back with Randi before anyone realizes what's going on."

The place was packed with G.L.O.W. Girls and G.L.O.W. Girl leaders. I saw Mom, Dad, and Teddy seated way down front. On the stage, sitting on chairs behind a podium, were Ms. Morgan and Randi, who was wearing my uniform and glasses. Everyone seemed to be waiting for something.

"Look over there," Wormy said as he tapped my shoulder and pointed at the back of the room. There stood Jay-Jay and Bobbi Joy.

"Great," I muttered. "This is some fix. I'm out here, and Randi is in there. Good-bye, merit badge."

I watched Randi onstage. She fumbled with my glasses. She looked pretty worried.

"Don't your parents know that Randi isn't you?" Wormy asked.

I shook my head. "We look so much alike that sometimes we can fool even them," I replied. "But once Randi opens her mouth, they'll know who is who." I stared silently through the window. I had to think of something—but what?

"You don't have to stand out here you know," someone behind us said. "This speech is open to the public."

Wormy and I turned around. Ms. Crump was standing right behind us.

"Randi Daniels," she said. "You don't have to watch Sandi's speech from the window. Come on. I'll squeeze you and your friend in somehow."

Before I could say anything, Ms. Crump took me by the hand and led me toward the front door of the building. Wormy followed. There was no escape. We were trapped.

Ms. Crump pulled me into the building. Wormy closed the door behind us, and we stood at the rear of the room. Nobody noticed us except Ms. Morgan.

"Ah, there's Ms. Crump now," said Ms. Morgan as she got to her feet. She walked up to the microphone. "Now we can begin our special presentation."

Everyone clapped. When the applause died down, Ms. Morgan continued. "Today, Sandi Daniels, one of the G.L.O.W. Girls in my group, will present a guest lecture on the native wildlife of Lake Kickapoo. Sandi also will receive the wildlife expert merit badge. I know all of you understand what a great achievement this is."

Everyone clapped again. "Now, without further delay, I present G.L.O.W. Girl Sandi Daniels."

"We're doomed," I whispered to Wormy. "Randi hates speaking in front of an audience."

I saw Randi gulp onstage. She took a deep breath and picked up my briefcase, which was on the floor beside her chair. Slowly, she walked toward the podium. When she put the briefcase down flat on the speaker's stand, the room got quiet. I could tell she didn't know what to do next.

"T-today, I-I'm going to talk about, uh, wildlife," said Randi very softly. The crowd began to buzz.

"B-before I begin," she sputtered, "I need my notes."

I heard Randi click open the locks on the briefcase. She opened the briefcase slowly. SPRONG! RIBBET! Out jumped Hoppy. The big bullfrog leaped from the podium out into the middle of the stage.

The crowd gasped. And then they burst into laughter. The whole room went bonkers!

"Goodness!" cried Ms. Morgan as she lunged at the frog.

RIBBET! croaked Hoppy in alarm. He escaped Ms. Morgan by jumping off the stage into the main aisle between all the chairs.

Girls shrieked! Boys hollered! Parents shouted. One little boy—I don't think I need to tell you who—cried out, "Dat my froggie!"

"Stop that frog!" cried Randi as she took off my glasses and jumped off the stage. "Don't

let him get away!"

A girl in the audience made a grab for Hoppy. But she missed. Somebody's father tried to throw his hat over Hoppy. But he missed, too. The meeting was turning into a three-ring circus. What a monstrous mess up!

RIBBET! RIBBET! Hoppy went bouncing up the aisle as shocked G.L.O.W. Girls screamed and laughed.

Teddy scooted away from Mom and Dad and went charging after Hoppy. Randi raced after Teddy. Mom, Dad, and Ms. Morgan went after Randi. It was like a goofy follow-the-leader game.

"I'll get that frog!" yelled Wormy as he ran down the center aisle to meet Hoppy.

"I'll help you!" Jay-Jay shouted as he pushed through the crowd.

The boys dove for the frog at the same time. But both were better fishermen than frog catchers. Hoppy jumped up and away from them and toward me. He tried to get around me, but I was too quick for him. I grabbed that slippery lump of croaking green slime and held him tight! The circus was over. But the worst was yet to come.

When I looked up, Mom, Dad, Ms. Morgan, Ms. Crump, Randi, and Teddy were standing around me.

"Hi, Sanee," said Trouble. "Dat my froggie. I did what you say. I put Hoppy in a safe place."

Leave it to Teddy to blab to the world which twin was which.

I nodded. "Good boy, Teddy," I said as I gave him his frog. He smiled. But no one else was smiling.

Dad glared at Randi, who was dressed in my uniform. She sighed. Then Dad looked at me. "All right. Which one of you is going to tell me what's going on?" he demanded.

"I'll tell you what's going on," Mom said. "It's the old switcheroo. Why did you do it?"

I tried to swallow but my throat was too dry. "It's a long story, Mom," I said sighing.

The crowd was starting to get restless.

"If you're Sandi," Ms. Morgan said pointing at me. "Then you're...," she pointed at my sister.

"I'm Randi," Randi admitted.

"I think I want to hear this long story," said Ms. Crump.

"So do I," Bobbi Joy said as she pushed her way into our group.

"We all want to hear this," Dad said.

"Right," agreed Ms. Morgan. "But first I have to dismiss this assembly. One thing's for sure, no merit badge is going to be awarded today." She walked back to the stage to dismiss the G.L.O.W. Girl gathering.

"I'm sorry, Sandi," said Randi. "I guess things didn't work out very well."

"Don't worry about it now," I said to Randi. I was upset about the merit badge. But I was more worried about how I was going to explain everything to Mom and Dad.

Twelve

R ANDI, Wormy, and I stood there silently as everyone walked past. Soon the room was empty except for the Daniels family, Wormy, Ms. Morgan, and Ms. Crump.

"Now," said Dad, "who wants to start to explain?"

RIBBET! croaked Hoppy, squirming in Teddy's hands.

"That frog has caused enough trouble," Dad said. "Put him back in the briefcase, Teddy."

"Otay," answered Teddy. He walked to the stage and put the frog back in the briefcase.

Dad asked again, "Now how did this all start?"

I looked at Randi. Randi looked at me. "It

all started with a skunk," we both said at the same time.

"A skunk?" asked Ms. Morgan.

"A skunk," Randi repeated. "Tell them, Sandi."

I began to explain. It started with Randi getting sprayed while she was waiting for Wormy. I went over all the details of my fishing trip, including the big lake trout and all the activity at the weigh-in.

"You mean we won the derby?" Randi cried out.

"We sure did!" Wormy said. "Wait until you see our trophy! And you should have seen that lake trout. It's the biggest one ever caught in Lake Kickapoo!"

"Kickaphew! Phew!" called Teddy. He was walking up the aisle dragging the closed briefcase behind him.

"Not now, Teddy," said Dad.

I continued. "All the picture taking made me late getting home. When I got there everyone was already gone." I looked at Randi.

"Well, I couldn't let Sandi miss her chance to earn that merit badge," Randi blurted out. "She had helped me. So, I had to help her. I guess I goofed. I'm sorry."

"We both goofed," I admitted. "I'm sorry, too. I guess we goof up every time we switch places."

"That's for sure," said Mom with a little chuckle.

"It's not funny," Dad said. "I mean it's funny, but it's not that funny. I'll have to think of some kind of punishment—later." And then Dad let out a little laugh, too.

Ms. Morgan looked at Ms. Crump. They started laughing, too. "Well, what you did was wrong," said Ms. Morgan. "But I think we all understand why you did it."

Randi and I nodded.

"I feel bad about Sandi's merit badge," sighed Randi. "She really worked hard for it. And her speech was so good."

"I think we might be able to reschedule her

speech for next week," Ms. Crump said. "What do you think, Ms. Morgan?"

"That sounds fair," Ms. Morgan agreed. "And it also sounds like Sandi might qualify for the fishing merit badge."

"Oh, that's great!" I cried.

Ms. Crump and Ms. Morgan nodded. I smiled. "One thing I learned from all of this is that fishing can be fun," I said.

"And I learned something, too," added Randi. "Being a G.L.O.W. Girl might be fun, too."

"You can join any time you want," Ms. Crump told Randi. "Just see me about filling out an application form."

"It looks like this story is going to have a happy ending, after all," said Wormy as we all walked toward the door.

But when we opened the door, the happy ending went up in smoke.

Blocking our path was Bobbi Joy.

"I was listening at the window," Bobbi Joy

said. "I heard everything. If Sandi substituted for Randi in the fishing derby, that's against the rules."

"You're right, Bobbi Joy," I said. "We broke the rules. You and Jay-Jay won."

"We'll tell the judges all about the mistake," added Randi.

"You won't have to," snapped Bobbi Joy. "I'll do it for you." And she walked off.

"Does this mean I have to give back the trophy?" asked Wormy.

"Yes, Wormy," Mom said sadly. "I guess it does."

Wormy shrugged his shoulders. "Oh, well, it's no big deal. This is the most fun I've had in years!"

We drove down to the lake. Wormy and Dad tied Wormy's canoe onto the roof of our station wagon. Then we all piled into the car and headed for the town hall.

"This sure is a nice trophy," Randi said, holding the trophy she'd have to give back.

"It'll look great in Bobbi Joy's bedroom, won't it?" I asked.

"Yeah," Randi answered. "But at least you still have the record fish."

"That's right," agreed Wormy. "All they have to do is put the name Sandi instead of Randi in the record book."

"Here we are," Dad announced as he parked in front of the town hall.

"Do you want us to go in with you?" Mom asked.

"No," I answered. "We made this mess, so we'll straighten it out."

Mom smiled and nodded at us.

Wormy, Randi, and I went in and explained everything to the judges. As we were walking back out the door, Randi said, "Well, I guess that's all over with."

"Not quite," I muttered. "Look over there."

Standing next to a tree were Jay-Jay and Bobbi Joy.

"I wish this had turned out differently,"

Jay-Jay said as we walked up to them. "I hope there are no hard feelings. We're still friends, aren't we?"

I smiled at Jay-Jay. "Sure," I said. "See you later."

"Ahem," said Bobbi Joy. "There's just one more thing. I'll stop by your cabin tomorrow morning so Randi can pay off on our bet."

"Right," replied Randi through gritted teeth. "See you tomorrow."

Thirteen

THE next morning, Randi, Wormy, and I sat on the porch of the cabin waiting for Bobbi Joy to show up. Randi had on her favorite red jumpsuit. She said a jumpsuit was the perfect thing to wear for jumping in a lake.

Suddenly, the cabin door opened. "Is she here yet?" Dad asked, poking his head out.

"Here comes Bobbi Joy now," Wormy announced. He pointed at the path that led out of the woods. "And Jay-Jay's with her, too."

"I might as well get this over with," Randi said as she started down the steps.

"Ranee gonna get a soaker," sang Teddy.

"Teddy, not now," I said.

"Are you ready?" Bobbi Joy asked.

"I'm as ready as I'll ever be," Randi said.

"Wait for us," Dad called as he, Mom, and Teddy stepped out of the cabin. Together we all went down the stairs after Randi.

"Hi, Jay-Jay," I greeted. "Are you here to watch Randi's soaker?"

"Actually, I came to ask you to go fishing with me this afternoon." He blushed a bit as if he were embarrassed. "I thought it would be fun if you and I and Randi and Wormy all went fishing together."

"That sounds super," I said. "And you know what? I'll even tell you guys the secret bait I used to catch that lake trout. But you won't believe it."

"I'll believe it," said Wormy. "I saw it work with my own eyes."

Mom, Dad, Teddy, Jay-Jay, Wormy, and I waited and watched. Bobbi Joy and Randi stood eye to eye and nose to nose. They were right at the water's edge.

"Okay, Randi," said Bobbi Joy. "It's time to

pay up on our bet."

"One! Two! Three!" Randi counted. And then she jumped into the water with a giant splash!

We all laughed at Randi, who was standing waist-deep in Lake Kickapoo. "Are you happy now, Bobbi Joy?"

"I sure am," she answered. "Only a nerd would jump into a lake with her clothes on."

Suddenly, Teddy started to yell. "Look! It's my kitty! My kitty came back. Here kitty, kitty!"

We all turned around. Waddling down the path right toward us was the skunk. And there was no place for us to run. We were trapped between the skunk and the lake!

"What do we do?" sputtered Bobbi Joy.

"There's only one thing to do," Dad replied as he picked up Teddy. "Into the lake, everyone!" KA-SPLASH! We all jumped into the lake, clothes and all. Only one person didn't jump. Bobbi Joy just stood there as the skunk came closer and closer.

"Jump, Bobbi Joy!" Mom yelled.

"Jump! Jump quickly!" Jay-Jay screamed. "You know what a skunk can do!"

"YEOW!" screamed Bobbi Joy as she leaped into the water. She landed with a tremendous splash that frightened the skunk away. I never saw an animal run so fast.

Bobbi Joy came up for air, sputtering and splashing.

"Hey," said Randi. "Do you know what? Losing this bet didn't turn out half bad!"

We all laughed. All of us except for one person, that is.

"Grrr," grumbled Bobbi Joy as she splashed her way toward the shore. She climbed out of the water and headed up the path for her cabin. Then she turned around and shouted, "I hate Lake Kickapoo!"

"Lake Kickaphew! Phew! Phew!" Teddy yelled out as Bobbi Joy sloshed away in her squishy sneakers.

And then we all laughed some more!

About the Author

MICHAEL J. PELLOWSKI was born on January 24, 1949, in New Brunswick, New Jersey. He is a graduate of Rutgers, the State University of New Jersey, and has a degree in education. Before turning to writing he was a professional football player and then a high school teacher.

He is married to Judith Snyder Pellowski, his former high school sweatheart. They have four children, Morgan, Matthew, Melanie, and Martin. They also have two cats, Carrot and Spot, and a German shepherd named Spike.

Michael is the author of more than seventy-five books for children. He is also the host and producer of two local TV shows seen on cable TV in his home state. His children's comedy show, "Fun Stop," was nominated as one of the best local cable TV children's shows in America.